Best Friends Forever

A World War II Scrapbook

BY BEVERLY PATT

WITH ILLUSTRATIONS BY SHULA KLINGER

Louise + Dottie = BF4Ever

This Book Belongs To

Louise Margaret Krueger

In memory of my mother,
Joan S. Kretchmer Lyle, the first writer
I knew and the inspiration for this book

two lions

Amazon Publishing
Attn: Amazon Children's Publishing
P.O. Box 400818, Las Vegas, NV 89140
www.amazon.com/amazonchildrenspublishing

Every effort has been made to trace the copyright holders of any material included in this book.
We apologize for any omissions or errors in this regard and would be pleased to make the
appropriate acknowledgment in any future printings.

Thank you to the following for the use of historical photographs:

National Archives and Records Administration: page 7

Library of Congress, Prints & Photographs Division: page 12 [LC-USF33-013290-M3 (b&w film
neg.)] and page 17 [LC-USZ62-23602 (b&w film copy neg, original negative is at NARA)]

LIBRARY OF CONGRESS CATALOGING-IN-PUBLICATION DATA
Patt, Beverly. Best friends forever : a World War II scrapbook / by Beverly Patt. —1st ed p. cm.
Summary: Fourteen-year-old Louise keeps a scrapbook detailing the events in her life after her
best friend, a Japanese-American girl, and her family are sent to a relocation camp during
World War II. ISBN 978-1-4778-1045-3 1. Japanese Americans—Evacuation and relocation,
1942–1945—Juvenile fiction. [1. Japanese Americans—Evacuation and relocation, 1942–1945—
Fiction. 2. Puyallup Assembly Center (Puyallup, Wash.)—Fiction. 3. World War, 1939–1945—
United States—Fiction. 4. Friendship—Fiction. 5. Seattle (Wash.)—History—20th century—
Fiction.] I. Title. PZ7.P27569Be 2009 [Fic]—dc22 2008020875

BOOK DESIGN BY KRISTEN BRANCH   EDITOR: ROBIN BENJAMIN

Best Friends Forever

A WORLD WAR II SCRAPBOOK

BY BEVERLY PATT

WITH ILLUSTRATIONS BY SHULA KLINGER

two lions

APRIL 24, 1942

This is me, Louise Margaret Krueger, age 14. →

Terrible picture, I know. I was determined not to show my teeth (I've heard that makes your nose look longer), but my rotten brother made me laugh. Dirty trick, don't you agree?

This is Dottie Masuoka (also 14) and my very best friend.

Dottie is the reason I am starting this scrapbook. She left today, and I don't know when she'll return. The Masuokas and all the other Japanese families have to be "relocated" (Mother says "kidnapped") until the war is over. And not just here in the Seattle area. In all of Washington! California and Oregon, too. I wonder, will this spread to all forty-eight states?

Dottie promised to write, and I promised to write back. I also promised myself one more thing: I'd keep a record of everything that goes on while Dottie's away and share it with her when she returns.

I hope, for our sake, this turns out to be a very short scrapbook. ♡

APRIL 29, 1942

Pop's always after me to start at the beginning instead of jumping right into the muck of things. (Being a reporter for The Seattle Beacon, he's picky about how to tell a story.) So, backing up, here is how it all began:

The Seattle B

Monday, December 8, 1941

PEARL HARBOR ATTACKED!

Japan bombed airfields and torpedoed battleships yesterday morning, causing severe damage to the US Pacific fleet and taking many American lives. President Roosevelt is meeting with Congress to discuss plans of war.

Pop saved a bunch of these—he said they might be worth something one day. So of course, I saved one, too. Just because Japan bombed us, suddenly everyone believes Japanese people like the Masuokas are <u>spies</u>. Mr. Masuoka is an Accountant!

These handbills went up about a month ago (crumpled from being hidden in my pocket).

INSTRUCTIONS
TO ALL PERSONS OF
JAPANESE
ANCESTRY

Living on Bainbridge Island:

ALL JAPANESE PERSONS, BOTH ALIEN AND NON-ALIEN, WILL BE EVACUATED BY

12:00 O'CLOCK NOON, FRIDAY, APRIL 24TH, 1942

Provisions have been made to give temporary residence in a reception center elsewhere. Evacuees who do not go to an approved destination of their own choice, but who go to a reception center under Government supervision, must carry with them the following property, not exceeding that which can be carried by the family or individual:

BLANKETS AND LINENS FOR EACH MEMBER OF THE FAMILY;

TOILET ARTICLES FOR EACH MEMBER OF THE FAMILY;

CLOTHING FOR EACH MEMBER OF THE FAMILY;

SUFFICIENT KNIVES, FORKS, SPOONS, PLATES, BOWLS, AND CUPS FOR EACH MEMBER OF THE FAMILY;

ALL ITEMS CARRIED WILL BE SECURELY PACKAGED, TIED, AND PLAINLY MARKED WITH THE NAME OF THE OWNER AND NUMBERED IN ACCORDANCE WITH INSTRUCTIONS RECEIVED AT THE CIVIL CONTROL OFFICE;

NO CONTRABAND ITEMS MAY BE CARRIED.

So they're being rounded up and evacuated to who-knows-where. But maybe getting away from all these crazy people will be good for the Masuokas. Last week, Dicky Grecko tripped Dottie in the hall and called her a "dirty Jap." I used to think Dicky was dreamy. Now he's the biggest creep I know.

APRIL 30, 1942

The last movie Dottie and I saw together—Blue, White and Perfect. Marion Hunter went, too. It was a detective movie (which I usually love), but the bad guys were a Nazi smuggling ring. Can't we forget about the war for just an hour? But then again, it's impossible to forget, now that Dottie is gone. Where is she? When will I hear from her?

MAY 1, 1942

Today is May Day, and Dottie missed it. I'm going to write her all about it in my first letter. She's going to miss Confirmation, too. It's not fair! We were going to do all these things <u>together</u>. Only the 8th graders get to be Maypole dancers, and Confirmation only comes around once as well.

My hair ribbon from the dance.

May Day is all about celebrating spring and flowers, so I wore my blue sundress, even though my heart feels more like winter. Here is how it went: We all stood in a circle, boy-girl-boy-girl, each holding a ribbon. Then when the music began, we wove in and around each other, boys going one way, girls the other, until our ribbons were all used up. Some people say the boy you end up closest to will be your future husband. Dicky Grecko ended up at my elbow. When he grinned at me, I <u>accidentally</u> ground my heel into his foot.

Program from the May Day Performance.

WASHINGTON JUNIOR HIGH SCHOOL

WELCOMES YOU TO THEIR ANNUAL

MAY DAY PERFORMANCE
MAY 1, 1942

MRS. BETTY LANNON, MUSICAL DIRECTOR

MAY 2, 1942

From last week's paper (Finally! Pop wouldn't let me cut anything out until now.):

Another train like the one that took Dottie away. The whole scene felt so eerie. The train station is usually such a happy place filled with people wearing their Sunday best, chatting excitedly, and hugging and kissing (even when they're saying good-byes). But not this time.

First of all, because no one knew much about where they were going, the outfits ranged from their Sunday best to winter wear and everything in between. One older woman sat on a bench, perspiring under seven or eight layers of clothes. (That's one good way to get around the two-bags-per-person rule! If you don't pass out, that is.) And while there were smiles, they were the forced kind, where the eyes didn't match the up-turned mouths. This was the hardest to see—this pretend cheerfulness—and hearing people assure their friends, "Don't worry! We'll be fine."

But will they?

We found the Masuokas right before they boarded. Dottie looked happy to see us, but her parents and grandfather looked embarrassed. They shouldn't be—they didn't do anything wrong. Dottie didn't cry. But I did. Everyone had to wear a tag with their family's number on it. It's like they're luggage, not people.

Maybe when we find out where they're living, we can go and visit.

MAY 3, 1942

MY FIRST LETTER FROM DOTTIE!!!

April 29, 1942

Dear Louise,

Guess what? Remember when your parents took us to the Western Washington State Fair in Puyallup last year? Well, that is where we are living! Only now it looks awful. Instead of popcorn stands and gaily painted game booths, rows of ugly shacks fill the old fairgrounds and we live in them, one small room per family. [Now I see why we couldn't bring pets—there's barely room for us!] Our "homes" are all attached in long lines, so we're like horses in stalls [except horses don't have to share their stalls]. The walls stop about 4 feet below the ceiling, so we can hear everything that goes on in our neighbors' stalls! There are so many rows that each time I go to the bathroom, it takes me ages to find my way back. Our mattresses are stuffed with hay, too. Daddy told me that some families here are living in real horse stalls, so I keep my complaints to myself. To cheer us up, he hung my Art League Blue Ribbon Winner right next to his bed. [You remember it—the painting with the sailboats and Bainbridge Island in the background?]

The only good part is seeing the roller coaster in the distance and remembering the fun you and I had there.

The other thing that's different is that we can't leave—the whole place is wrapped in barbed wire and surrounded by guard towers. It's just as crowded as the fair, only all the people have sad faces—sad Japanese faces. I never knew there were so many Japanese people in the whole universe, let alone Washington State. Last night, I heard the old woman next door, Mrs. Yatsushiro, crying. She's been here a week and just got a letter from home saying that all her china stored in her neighbor's garage was stolen. Doesn't that beat all? As if leaving it behind weren't bad enough.

I miss you and Roxy so much, I could burst. Thank you for watching her for me—tell her she must be a good puppy and not chew your mother's nice couch.

Whinny snicker snort (that's horse language for <u>Write back soon</u>).

Dottie

My new address:
Camp Harmony
Area A, Block 4
Puyallup, Washington

P.S. I don't know who came up with the name Camp Harmony—it's more like Camp Discord at the moment.
P.P.S. Tell your brother that my cousin Albert says hello.

OUR "APARTMENT"

Mrs. Y Snoring! ZZZZZZ ← 4 foot gap

←Stove Pipe

Chair made of scraps

picture from Dottie

Barbed wire? I take back what I said earlier, about this possibly being a good thing for the Masuokas. How could living behind barbed wire ever be a good thing? When we sing "The Star-Spangled Banner" at school, the last line really sticks in my throat. O'er the land of the free and the home of the brave? Well, Dottie and her family sure are brave. But they're definitely not free.

I remember the night before the state fair. I could barely sleep—both from excitement as well as from the pin curls Mother made me wear to bed. My head aches just thinking of it. Boy, did Dottie and I have fun, though. We rode the carousel, the Coaster Thrill ride, and the merry-go-round. We even jitterbugged in the Dance Hall until two men with a huge, braided rope practically lassoed us off the floor. Adults only. Phooey. (Dottie tried to duck under the rope but got caught!) It's hard to believe Dottie is living in the fairgrounds now.

I can't stop thinking about ladylike Mrs. Masuoka sleeping on a smelly hay mattress. To quote Mother, "It's inexcusable."

MAY 5, 1942

Roxy's footprint, 3 months old.

She's a Wirehair Terrier and cute as the day is long. But nothing is safe from her sharp puppy teeth. She chewed Mother's slip while it hung on the clothesline! We have a lot to learn about raising a puppy. Werner calls her a pain in the neck, but at night I hear him talking to her in the kitchen before he goes to bed. My brother's not so tough.

MAY 7, 1942

All the stores owned by the Japanese are empty and boarded up now. (Before, some owners hung signs like this to show their loyalty and to stop possible looters.) People had to sell or give away or put in storage everything they owned, except what they could carry with them to the camps. Mother heard that many

Page

WHITE & POLLARD

GROCERY   WA

FRUITS
AND
VEGETABLES

I AM AN AMERICAN

WANTO CO   WANTO CO

Japanese burned family heirlooms, photos, and anything that looked "too Japanese" to avoid appearing disloyal to America. Pop offered to store the Masuokas' car in our garage, but Mr. M said he didn't want to be a burden. He sold his 1941 Studebaker for $50, though it was worth much more. Mr. Nishiyama, the fruit stand man, made a bonfire and burned all his antique furniture rather than sell it for pennies. He burned his stand, too. We will miss him and his delicious pears.

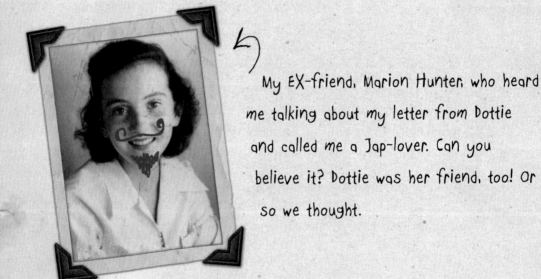

My EX-friend, Marion Hunter, who heard me talking about my letter from Dottie and called me a Jap-lover. Can you believe it? Dottie was her friend, too! Or so we thought.

My SECOND letter from Dottie!!! I wrote once already, but it looks like she didn't receive my letter yet.

May 2, 1942

Dear Louise,

Just my luck to spend 1 and 3/4 torturous years at Washington Junior High, only to miss being one of the dancers on May Day. Was it wonderful? Which boy did you end up standing next to? Here is a painting of how I imagined it. You are the one in blue.

I can't believe I'm going to miss being confirmed, too. It's so unfair! I am missing everything. But Cousin Albert and his classmates here are missing their high school graduation, which is definitely worse. We're told they'll receive their diplomas in the mail. My uncle Taro is organizing a makeshift ceremony for all the seniors in the camp, and Aunt Etsu has invited the family over to her "home" for tea (made on an unauthorized hot plate! Shh! But everyone's got one). She'll also be serving cookies (made in her real home) that she brought to camp just for this occasion. They'll probably be rock hard! At least it's something.

Some bad news—my grandfather is doing poorly. He just sits in our little apartment and stares out the one small window. He even refuses to eat. (Although I can't blame him—they drown our rice in apricot juice—ugh.) Being around Grandpa makes me sadder, so I mostly stay outside. By watching and listening, I have found out many camp secrets: the fleet-footed Komata brothers grab second and third meals at Mess Halls across camp, one guy (I can't say his name because they might read our letters) snuck an engagement ring into camp by hiding it in his mouth, and old Mrs. Yatsushiro uses the latrine only when the rest of the camp is at dinner!

And speaking of Mrs. Y, guess what? Mama volunteered me to keep her company every day while the rest of her family are at their camp jobs! Mrs. Y is shorter than me and about a thousand years old. She looks terribly frail but she can talk the ears off a rabbit, especially on the subject of Young People and Their Shameful Lack of Japanese Manners. She has decided it is her mission in life to teach me every prehistoric Japanese custom she knows.

Even though Mr. Y and his grown son work all day in the dust, patching together a Recreation building, and the son's wife sweats it out in the Mess Halls washing dishes, I'd gladly switch places with any of them to get away from Mrs. Y.

Lou Lou, I am in a prison <u>inside</u> a prison. Please write soon!

Best Friends Forever,
Dottie

P.S. They call bathrooms "latrines" here. Toilets all in a row— no walls between! Showers are the same way. We girls are used to it, after taking swimming at the YWCA. But the older women think it's humiliating. I think I saw Mrs. Okuro crying in the shower the other day. But maybe it was just the water. Across camp, some men used wood scraps to build private stalls in two women's latrines. I hear the lines for those are longer than the horizon (which, if you'd paid attention in Art class, you'd know goes on forever. Ha, ha!).

You!

You can tell Art is Dottie's favorite subject. But not mine. I can never see the point of drawing all those silly pictures of fruit bowls—especially when there's a Nancy Drew book to read! Of course, I'm forever getting caught reading instead of drawing in class, making me Miss Murret's least favorite Art student. Well, she's my least favorite teacher, so we're even.

Dottie guessed I wore my blue dress! (Of course, I only own three dresses.)

MAY 10, 1942

My Confirmation certificate. Mother surprised me this morning with a beautiful dress she made out of dotted swiss!

confirmation ✝ certificate

This certifies that

Louise Margaret Krueger

having received a thorough instruction in the sacred teachings
of the Christian religion as found in the Holy Scriptures and confessed by the

LUTHERAN CHURCH

and having vowed before God and this Christian congregation
to be faithful unto our Lord Jesus Christ and His saving Gospel

was received into communicant membership in

Saint Andrew's Lutheran Church
at Bainbridge Island, Washington

by the solemn rite of

CONFIRMATION

on the 10th day of May , A.D. 19 42

Pastor William Mael, Th. D.
PASTOR

dotted swiss

I didn't even mind wearing my old anklet socks with it. Then, wouldn't you know, Marion Hunter showed up at the church in <u>real</u> silk stockings. Imagine! Her father must have bought them off the black market.

To make matters worse, Marion recited <u>Dottie's</u> scripture verse, Luke 4:18, about preaching good news to the poor, giving sight back to the blind, and releasing the prisoners and the oppressed. But stupid Marion mixed it all up, saying to preach the good news to the <u>prisoners</u>, give sight back to the <u>poor</u>, and release the <u>blind</u>. Dottie had it memorized for months. Isn't it strange that Dottie's verse talked about releasing prisoners, and now she's sort of a prisoner herself?

The ceremony was nice, but I couldn't concentrate. I kept thinking of the guard towers that Dottie mentioned. Which direction are their guns pointing—out? Or in? It was also hard to pay attention to Pastor Mael's sermon with Marion sitting right next to me, admiring her new silk hose. The only thing I remember is a phrase he kept repeating—pray <u>without ceasing</u>. But how do you do that? And wouldn't you run out of things to pray for?

As we were leaving, Marion tripped and sprained her ankle. The way she carried on, you'd think she'd fractured it. I know it sounds mean, but it serves her right for calling me a Jap-lover. I only wish she'd ripped her hose as well!

MAY 18, 1942

A seed packet from our new Victory Garden.

We are growing our own vegetables, so the farmers can ship theirs to our soldiers overseas. I have 2 blisters on one hand and 3 on the other from digging and planting. Pop says it's good for me. I say, it hurts!

Here is the layout of our garden.

Hey, wouldn't Miss Murret be pleased to see this? But I'm not going to show her. This scrapbook is only for me and Dottie, when she comes home. When will that be, I wonder? She has been gone twenty-four whole days and I am miserable. I'm going to ask Pop if we can visit very, very soon.

Tomatoes

Pole Beans

Carrots

Bibb lettuce

Beets (Yuck)

Cabbage (double Yuck)

Red Potatoes

Zucchini

May 16, 1942

Dear Louise,

Mrs. Y gave me sitting lessons today—<u>seiza</u>, it's called in Japanese—and I don't think I'll ever get the feeling back in my legs. She's a tyrant: <u>Hands on lap! Fingers together! Toes flat! Back straight!</u> I'm thinking of recommending her to the army. She'd make a great sergeant. But she'd have a devil of a time keeping her kimono clean. Ha, ha.

And speaking of the army, Cousin Albert and all his buddies constantly talk about proving their loyalty to America by volunteering for the war. They are not allowed—not yet, anyway. Even Japanese men who were serving in the military <u>before</u> the war broke out have been taken off active duty. Do you know what the army calls them? "4C—Enemy Alien."

Daddy thinks it's just a matter of time before the War Department changes its mind and begins recruiting our boys. He made the mistake of saying so the other night when my aunt and uncle were over. My uncle started saying things like, "Over my dead body!" Aunt Etsu just bent farther over the curtains she was sewing and didn't say a word. Mother waved at our four very-close walls. "Look where we are living," she said. "They wouldn't have the nerve to ask our boys to serve." Then Grandpa put in <u>his</u> two cents. It was the first I'd heard him talk in weeks. (I didn't catch all of it because it was in Japanese, and I understood only some of the words.) Aunt Etsu came to life, shushing Grandpa, saying he'll be arrested for being disloyal (which was actually pretty funny considering we already live in a camp with guns pointing at us—but no one laughed). It became a big argument, ending with Aunt Etsu and Mother in tears, Uncle Taro foaming at the mouth, Grandpa still muttering in Japanese, and my father suddenly deciding he needed to go find scrap wood to build a table.

Enough about that. Thank you for your letters! I cannot believe Marion not only <u>has</u> stockings but <u>wears</u> them. She is such a show-off. Who does she think she is? I have to admit, I was happy about her fall, too! But, Louise, you left out the most important news—who did the Maypole say you are supposed to marry? Hopefully not Russell Sneedman, with his perpetually runny nose! But even if it did, I will still be your maid of honor. And I will throw tissues instead of rice.

Write back soon.

XO, Dottie

P.S. Here's me during Mrs. Y's sitting lessons. Next thing you know, she'll be teaching me to walk and talk. Ha! How do you like my new haircut? Not very glamorous but easier to care for in this mud pit.

P.P.S. Camp Harmony is now like a small city. It includes: Area A housing, Post Office, Bank, Recreation Hall (Ping-Pong and baseball are the most popular pastimes), Clinic, Canteen (where you can buy small things like toothbrushes, soap, thread, etc.). It's easy to get lost! (Can you tell I'm bored? There's nothing else to do but draw these pictures.)

MAY 22, 1942

Dottie's and my favorite actress, Joan Fontaine.

We saw her in <u>Suspicion</u>—she won the Academy Award for Best Actress. After the movie, Dottie and I spent the whole afternoon imitating her fainting scene. We had to stop when I hit my head on the dresser and bled all over my good sweater (very un-Joan-Fontaine-like). Even though it hurt like heck, Dottie and I couldn't stop cracking up! Gosh, do I miss her.

JUNE 6, 1942

Two weeks since my last entry—mostly due to extra schoolwork and tests. It's like the teachers are trying to cram our heads with enough information to last us the whole summer! Look who's a High School Graduate! My brother, Werner Francis Krueger, BMOC (Big Man on Campus). Here is his graduation photo.

My friend Nancy Cortino says he looks dreamy, but I think he looks just like himself—a big, wavy-haired tease. If he's not calling me Little Miss Scaredy Pants, he's hanging my new brassiere on our door knocker. He's insufferable! In the fall, he will be studying Engineering at the University of Washington. Pop is bursting with pride, because U of W is his alma mater.

June 1, 1942

Dear Louise,

You're not going to believe this: Mrs. Y really IS teaching me how to walk! She lays out straw mats (tatami), which I have to shuffle across—Slow down! No noise! Good posture!—being careful not to step on the cracks between the mats. (Maybe I'll break my mother's back?!)

Where is Wonder Woman when you need her? Here's my version of Wonder Woman, but a little more sporty!

Daddy has been elected Personnel Officer of our Block, which means he has to go to each apartment to take roll at 9:00 a.m. and 9:30 p.m. (Right before the 10:00 p.m. curfew!) There are over 250 people in our Block. Can you imagine being counted twice a day? Just where do they think we will go? I'm proud he was elected but worried, too. What if he loses his way at night and gets close to the fence? The guards are on orders to shoot anyone who comes too close. How close is too close? I can't get to sleep until I hear his oxfords scuff across our sandy floor.

Oh gosh, it's lights out already. Darn! I shouldn't have spent so much time drawing.

Shuffle, scuffle, oops! (Japanese walking language for Send help quick!).

Dottie

P.S. Speaking of Wonder Woman, Cousin Albert says WW is going to have her OWN comic book— Coming Soon to a Store Near You. Keep your eyes peeled!

Step on a crack...

I know Dottie thinks they're hideous, but I think Mrs. Y's lessons sound elegant, like Princess Lessons. Maybe when Dottie gets home, she can teach me.

JUNE 14, 1942

Now here's something you don't see every day.

It's shrapnel, given to me by Seaman Nick Rossi, a soldier I met at Sasser Facial Rehab Hospital. He had a whole jarful that doctors had taken out of his eyes, face, and chest. (Oh, dear, here I go, getting ahead of myself again. Let me start over. . . .)

Pop was asked to write a story on the soldiers at Sasser for his job. After doing my best begging, he finally said I could go with him. He got special permission for me to write letters home for the injured soldiers—they would dictate and I would write. I was so excited and felt very grown-up the whole way there. But when the head nurse led me into the ward, I almost fainted. Some of their injuries were so horrible—entire parts of their faces missing—that I had to sit down in the nearest chair. I ended up writing only one letter (Nick's) before vomiting into a bedpan.

Both Nick's eyes were bandaged, so I'm not sure if he caught on to how upset I was. Gosh, I hope not. To make it worse, Nick's letter was so upbeat, never mentioning his injuries, just assuring his parents that he was fine and not to worry. I was actually crying as I wrote. I hope his parents are able to read it—my handwriting was terribly shaky.

On the way out, I passed a room where they make fake eyeballs for men who have lost one (or two). There were trays and trays of them: blue, green, brown. I thought I'd be sick again, but I had nothing left. Maybe Werner is right. Maybe I _am_ Miss Scaredy Pants.

JUNE 17, 1942

School's out—hooray! But without Dottie, I'm already bored. The most exciting thing I've done today is mix up the oleo. . . .

4 QUARTER-POUND PRINTS

SPRING'S BEST

YELLOW

VEGETABLE
OLEOMARGARINE

Butter is now rationed so we have to use oleo. Each white slab of oleo comes with a packet of orange powder. It's my job at home to mix in this orange coloring to fool us into thinking it's butter. But one taste, and you know it's not. I now eat my toast dry or with last year's homemade raspberry preserves.

Well, this day is looking up. A letter from Camp Harmony.

June 12, 1942

Dear Louise,

I never want to see the color brown again, even if I live to be one hundred. We've tramped down the last traces of grass, so that brown is the color of everything here—mud, walls, floors—and on dry days, even the sky is filled with brown dust. At least my paintings cover our walls. The camp is as boring as its color. There's nothing to do—besides Mrs. Y's torture for me. (Although, I must admit, Mrs. Y said my circulation would improve the more I sat seiza and it's true. I can now last 12 whole minutes before losing all feeling in my legs.) I've played so many games of marbles, I've actually developed a callous on my shooter finger. And believe it or not, I've even begun collecting and trading baseball cards. Me, the strikeout queen of Washington Junior High! It's something to do.

Oh! Remember Robert Fujiu? (Silly me—of course you do. But sometimes it seems like I've been gone for years instead of weeks.) Anyway, Robert lives a few stalls, I mean, apartments down and yesterday he said, "Don't you wish they had a school here?" Ha, ha! The boy who was always in the principal's office! Proof that the boredom is driving people bananas. Robert may soon get his wish. Yesterday I saw a sign on the Mess Hall door, asking for volunteer teachers.

Lou Lou, this place is horrible, but if I let out one peep, Daddy yells, "Shikata ga nai!" which means "It cannot be helped," or "Make the best of it." It's like the battle cry here. The only person I know who doesn't chant it is Grandpa. We have that in common, but you'd never know it. He has changed so much.

Remember how close we were, always working in his flower garden together? Not anymore. Now when he talks, all he can do is criticize me, the way I dress, the way I talk, everything. It's like this whole war—and us being penned in here like a bunch of criminals—is my fault.

Mama reminds me who he's really mad at—President Roosevelt—but he can't say a word against him, for fear of being labeled "disloyal." (Troublemakers are sent to a separate camp, we hear, and I don't know what happens there.) Even knowing all that, it still hurts when Grandpa gives me the cold shoulder or says things like, "Does Cousin Albert know you steal his footwear?" (when I'm wearing my saddle shoes). I have taken to calling him Grumpa but only in my mind.

Yours 'til the hot dog barks,
Dottie

P.S. The adults are bored, too, so they're forming their own classes. Daddy was asked to teach bookkeeping, three times a week, in the Rec. Hall. At first he was embarrassed, seeing as so many people had to give up or sell off their shops back home. But these men all have such positive attitudes, declaring they will open up new shops when they get out and need to know how to do their own books properly. For this, he earns $8 a month. The pay for all Japanese workers here is a joke. Young men laying pipe earn $12 a month, and doctors earn the most at $19! But Daddy wouldn't dream of complaining—it would be impolite, he says. Honestly.

P.P.S. How is Roxy? I wonder if she even remembers me.

Dottie is right. Her father's pay is completely unfair. Look at this ad I found in the paper! Rotten.

BOOKKEEPER WANTED

PART-TIME
$85 PER MONTH

APPLY AT
NELSON FUNERAL
PAR[...]

I have to do something to cheer her up. I keep asking Pop if we can visit. SOON. He keeps saying, "Pleasure trips are out of the question." But what if he was to do a story on the camps. . . ?
Gotta go!

JUNE 22, 1942

Note from Nancy Cortino, another soon-to-be EX-friend?

Dear Louise,
 Marion says you are a Jap-lover. Is this true?
                    Your friend,
                         Nancy

P.S. If it's not true, would you like to go to the movies this Saturday? and maybe invite Werner? Marion says she can't go on account of her ankle. (although it has to be healed by <u>NOW</u>, don't you think?)

Doesn't that beat all? I felt like telling her to take a hike—she and Marion, both. And can you believe she had the nerve to ask me to invite Werner? As if he would be interested in an 8th-grade girl. (And a mean one, at that!)

When I showed this note to Mother, she was furious and told me that I "shouldn't even dignify this with a response." Then she attacked a stack of potatoes with her vegetable knife. The sound of her furious scraping filled the kitchen. Five potatoes later, she put down her knife and said, "It's times like these that separate the wheat from the chaff, Louise. You just make sure you stick with the wheat."

I didn't understand, so I looked up "chaff" in the dictionary: 1. The useless <u>dry leaves</u> <u>surrounding grains of wheat</u>, removed <u>during threshing</u>. 2. <u>worthless material; garbage</u>. The wheat is the good stuff, so I suppose she meant stick with the good, like Dottie. Which I aim to do.

JUNE 23, 1942

Dottie's Next Letter. She sounds so down in the dumps. Very unlike her.

June 19, 1942

Dear Louise,

Until today, I never knew I could hate someone I loved so much.

I tried to _shikata ga nai_ and cheer Grumpa up. I know he misses his garden terribly, so I painted a picture of his favorite flowers—Jacob's Ladder, Wooly Sunflowers, and Woodland Stars—under an American flag. Do you know what he did? Ripped it in half! "Why _American_ flag?" he yelled. "You are _Japanese_, Hana-chan!"

"No!" I yelled back. "I am AMERICAN! And my name is DOTTIE!"

Little did I know, Daddy was standing just outside the door, hearing me be disrespectful. The rest of the day, I had to sit inside, facing the plywood wall. To put salt on the wound, Mrs. Y poked her bony finger through one of the many large knotholes. She waggled it at me and yelled through the wall that I was shameful, ignoring my Japanese blood. When will they listen, Lou Lou? My blood is red, white, and blue!

Just before bedtime, Grumpa pointed out the window: "Look, Hana-chan, where your _American_ President has put you." I tried to argue that at least no one's calling us "dirty Japs" here. But he just waved me away like a pesky fly (which, by the way, outnumber us here by about 100 to 1).

I couldn't get to sleep after that. I kept thinking, Why _did_ my American President put me here? By the time I fell asleep, I still hadn't come up with an answer.

Bizz byzz buzz (pesky fly language for _From your pal_).

—Dottie

P.S. I love your letters and hearing what's going on in the normal world—it takes my mind off this awful place. Can you believe I've been gone almost two months? It feels so much longer. Maybe next time you can tell me about Abbott and Costello's new movie, if you've seen it by then. It's bound to be a gas, and I sure could use a laugh. Huge hugs to you and Roxy.

P.P.S. Thanks for the baseball cards—the edges are so nice, I should be able to make a swell trade, if I decide to. But maybe I'll just hang on to them and make the other kids drool. Ha, ha!

P.P.P.S. For your scrapbook—an article from our camp's newspaper. This is the adults' big beef—that kids eat at separate tables from their parents in the Mess Hall (which is much more fun, in my book!). Yes, we now have a newspaper—or newsletter, rather. And a mayor. And several baseball teams and all sorts of clubs. And while these are good because they keep spirits up and people busy, they also worry me. Each new team or club or street sign makes this place feel more and more permanent, like we're getting ready to stay here a long time.

CAMP HARMONY NEWS-LETTER

Vol. 1, No. 5

Older Residents Concerned for Family Life

THERE IS CONCERN among our older residents that camp life is taking its toll on our families. "With our traditional family meal abandoned," states one resident, "and no household chores or businesses to help at, our children are slipping away from us." Complaints about ill-mannered youths are cropping up in all areas of the camp. Parents should encourage their youngsters to spend more time in the home, perhaps helping their fathers build furniture or their mothers sew curtains. In this way, families can continue to keep an eye on their children's activities and attitudes.

I wonder if Pop has talked to his editor yet about doing a story on the camps? He said he's hesitant to ask because of the gas. (I just learned that gas rationing is also about conserving rubber for tires. Japan took over all the plantations in the Dutch East Indies where the US bought most of its rubber. So that's why there's a big push to donate anything rubber—old tires, raincoats, garden hoses, even bathing caps!) Anyway, if we do go, I will bring Dottie an enormous care package filled with all her favorite things. But I wish I could bring her home instead.

ABBOTT AND COSTELLO'S
RIO RITA
ADMIT ONE 25c

JUNE 27, 1942

I finally got to see Rio Rita. I went with Werner, but he ended up sitting in the back with his pals. Nancy Cortino was there and kept turning around, pulling at the corners of her eyes and whispering, "Ahh-so!" as if that made her look Japanese. She got the whole row of kids to do it with her. So what? I don't need her or Marion. I still have Dottie, the best friend ever.

I have to admit, though, being best friends with someone who's not around can sure get lonely.

JUNE 28, 1942

Guess what? Mother is teaching me to knit. We are making socks for the soldiers. I am going to send my first pair to Nick Rossi, the shrapnel soldier. His ward was very chilly. I wonder if he'll remember me? In one way, I hope he does and in another, I hope he doesn't. I was so immature that day. He had a very nice smile and a strong chin like Clark Gable's. I wonder what his eyes look like (and if he'll ever be able to see with them again?).

The new owners of the Masuokas' house are never home—the husband is a soldier and the wife works in the Boeing factory, making planes for the war—so the weeds in the garden are taking over. (Which gives me an idea . . .)

JUNE 29, 1942

News Flash: We got to see Dottie! It happened so fast. Pop finally asked to do a story on the Japanese at Puyallup and his editor agreed right away, giving him two extra gas coupons! Pop said we could all come along, but he couldn't guarantee we'd be allowed in. Even though the camp is only about 30 miles away, it took us over an hour driving from Seattle, traveling at "victory speed" for rationing (35 mph). I was so excited when I saw the top of the roller coaster, I started bouncing in the back seat. Roxy, on my lap, barked and pawed at the glass.

Werner elbowed me. "We're not going to the fair, you know."

And then we saw the guard towers. Pop pulled over and we all just stared.

Pop said, "Now listen, the main thing is to be supportive. Don't mention their old house or anything that will make them feel worse than they already do. We want them to know they still have friends at home."

"And that we think this is a travesty," Mother added.

We checked in at the guardhouse, but they wouldn't let us through the gate—not even Pop with his press badge! Someone ran to tell the Masuokas they had visitors while we stood at the fence and waited. The fairgrounds are huge, and the camp seemed to go for miles in all directions. Pop said the place could hold over 7,000 people. He also said this was just one of sixteen "assembly centers," which are temporary camps until the more permanent ones are built. More? Permanent?

At last, they came. It was awkward for the first few seconds. Pop put out his hand, as if to shake Mr. Masuoka's, but of course, the fence was there. So Pop quickly tipped his hat instead. When he did that, his press badge blew off his jacket and sailed straight over the fence! The Masuokas all chased it—even proper Mrs. Masuoka—and by the time Dottie snatched it up, both families were laughing and the ice was broken.

We paired off along the fence—the fathers, the mothers, Dottie's cousin Albert and Werner, and Dottie and me. Roxy was jumping and barking her head off. Dottie dropped to her knees to say hello. Roxy couldn't decide whether to lick or bark or wiggle, so she did all three. Dottie whispered, "She remembers me."

I'm ashamed to say, I felt a flicker of jealousy—I'd almost forgotten that Roxy isn't really my dog. But I said, "Of course Roxy remembers you. You're all she ever talks about!"

That made Dottie laugh and eased my guilt a little, too.

Then we just made small talk. Dottie brought me up to date on Robert Fujiu and his endless attempts to get her attention. I was so excited to talk to her, I babbled about everything from knitting socks for Nick Rossi to seeing Nancy at the movies. I was just about to tell her the "Ahh-so" part when I caught myself. Dottie's eyes widened. She said, "Nancy made fun of you because of me, didn't she?" I said no and talked about the movie instead. But Dottie got quiet. I kept glancing up at the guard towers, remembering what she'd said about getting too close to the fence. She noticed and explained the rules were different for the Visitors' Area. Still, it was hard to concentrate with guns pointing all around. I don't know how Dottie does it.

When Pop said it was time to go, part of me was relieved. Being outside the fence felt like I <u>agreed</u> with their being locked up. Like I was part of the group that put them there. But saying good-bye felt worse. I cried the whole way home.

It's not like any "camp" I've ever known—no forest, no lake, no cozy log cabins—only miles and miles of mud and buildings that look like oversized rabbit hutches. <u>Poor Dottie.</u>

Grass from outside Camp Harmony:

JULY 2, 1942

I was even more relieved to get this. It sounds like our visit really made their day. Hard as it was, it was worth it. (I wish she hadn't mentioned those mean hecklers, though. I was trying to forget them.)

June 30, 1942

Dear Louise,

Your family's visit was the best thing that's happened since we got here (even if it was through the fence). And you didn't even flinch when those horrible people drove by and called your family names, on account of us. I was almost happy to be inside the fence and out of their reach. I hope they didn't give you any more trouble on your drive home.

You were swell to bring me shoots from Grumpa's old flower garden. How did you ever dig them up without the new owners seeing you? I planted them already. You probably heard through the mother grapevine—Grandfather's lost so much weight, they've put him in the Infirmary. I didn't want to bring it up yesterday and ruin our visit. We're all worried sick. This garden just <u>has</u> to make him better. How clever you are!

The comic books and Nancy Drew mystery were also great surprises. Can you believe how carefully the guards paged through them all? As if you were trying to smuggle top-secret information in them. Too bad you didn't shove a recipe or two inside—they'd have confiscated those, and then maybe we would have gotten a decent meal for once!

I forgot to tell you that "Vacation School" has started, from 10 to noon and 2 to 4 each day. Different people teach us different things, and we sit on the floor and use Mess Hall benches for desks. There are over 300 students and 16 volunteer teachers. We are divided into age groups, but the 6th, 7th, and 8th graders are all together.

Robert Fujiu has gone mad: He sits in front, raises his hand, and even knows some answers! He still tries to catch my eye, but I ignore him. He is such a pest. But now he is a studious pest.

There are two good things about school—one is that we have "handicraft" class. Right now we are learning embroidery, which is fun. The second is that Mrs. Y's Torture Sessions are cut to one hour per day. Hooray! This week she is teaching me flower arranging, which I was actually excited about until I realized, in order to do it properly, we must sit seiza style again.

Since we have no flowers to arrange, we use dead sticks, branches, and pine cones, and we place them in a "vase" made of stones. All branches must point toward Heaven, Mrs. Y says. It's pretty in a rustic sort of way—I've drawn you a picture.

XXOO to you and Roxy [She is SO big now! Thanks for bringing her].

$$\begin{array}{r} U\ R\ 2\ Good \\ +\ \ \ \ 2\ B \\ \hline 4\ Gotten \end{array}$$

Dottie

P.S. When you go to church, could you light a candle for Grumpa? A Block has its own chapel [made from two horse stalls instead of one], but somehow a candle here doesn't seem like it would work as well as one lit in St. Andrew's.

P.P.S. Daddy says to thank your father again for the nails, extension cords, and scatter rugs. We are now the best-decked-out stall on the Block!

Roxy's baby tooth—the only one I've found.

I can't believe President Roosevelt made Dottie leave this little puppy behind.

Werner brought home a chocolate bar (a luxury!) to split, but was very secretive as to how he got it. My guess is Betty Thompson—she's been carrying a torch for Werner since grammar school. As we sat on the back porch steps, letting the chocolate melt in our mouths, Werner said he had another secret and did I want to know what it was? Did I! But then he got this funny look—real serious-like—and suddenly, I didn't want to know. I jumped up and ran to my room. Later, I apologized but he just shrugged me off, saying I was too young to know anyway.

Why am I such a baby?

JULY 3, 1942

I wrote Nick Rossi a letter! (And spritzed it with Mother's perfume. Shhh!) I still feel horrible about what happened at the Rehab Hospital but didn't mention it—too embarrassing. Instead I told him about myself and what it's like living on Bainbridge

Island. (Pop always says the best writing is in the details.) I enclosed his knitted socks, too—they came out a bit lumpy, and one is slightly longer than the other.

They look like this: →

Maybe they'll feel better than they look.

We have been saving our sugar rations to make a treat for Dottie's grand-father, and we finally have enough! My parents gave up sugar in their coffee, and Werner and I haven't had a homemade sweet in weeks. Today, Mother found a shop that had eggs—she bought four! We can't decide if we should use just a little sugar for a special 4th of July treat. I say no, but Werner says yes.

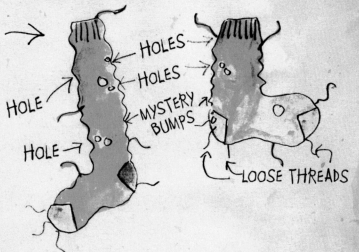

SAD, HOLEY SOCKS

HOLES
HOLES
HOLE
MYSTERY BUMPS
HOLE
LOOSE THREADS

JULY 7, 1942

Sounds like Dottie had as much fun on the 4th of July as I did.

July 4—Independence Day (but not for us)

Dear Louise,

Do you realize this is the first Fourth of July since kindergarten that we won't be together? Not that there will be any fireworks this year, seeing as all that explosive material is going toward ammunition. Camp Harmony is having a kiddie parade and a "concert" (playing borrowed records over the camp speakers). I can't decide if I will go or not. Maybe I'll just stay in and paint.

Which reminds me, there's a guy in our camp that won first prize in the National Defense poster contest! His name is Eddie Sato, and he's a really good artist. His poster is being printed in newspapers across the country! Why didn't I enter? It's strange, though—Eddie won a poster contest telling people to "Buy War Bonds," but he's a prisoner in the country he's supporting. The more I think about it, the more depressed I get.

Some days, Lou Lou, I don't speak a word to anyone. Every morning, I wake up with a fine layer of dust on me that has blown in through all the cracks in the walls. (The army used fresh wood, so now the planks are drying out and shrinking, leaving big gaps.) At first, we made a joke of it, saying it was expensive face powder. But it's getting harder and harder to laugh it off. We've tried filling the cracks and knotholes with old newspapers, but every day there are new cracks and new holes. Mother sweeps three times a day.

The food is terrible, school is a joke, I'm being beaten

down by a little old lady, and on top of all that, it's impossible to stay clean. (Imagine taking a shower and then drying off with a dusty towel. Ugh.) The worst part is feeling like a bird in a cage—never able to get out and go where you want. I think some of the guards actually feel bad about this whole mess. One guard by the baseball field earned the nickname "Home Run Hank" because of the way he cheers whenever someone hits it over the fence. He even threw down penny candy once, but rumor has it he got in trouble and hasn't done that since.

Every night I lie in bed, squeeze my eyes closed, and pretend I'm back at home. But the picture in my mind is getting fuzzy. And our home isn't even ours anymore. Oh, Lou Lou, why was I born with this Japanese face? No one can see my American heart.

Yours 'til the tree barks,
Dottie

P.S. Between the rain, scorching sun, and battering wind, Grumpa's garden is not looking great. (The ground is either gloppy mud or flaking dust.) He's still in the Infirmary and in spite of everything, I miss him. I'm praying for calm, temperate days ahead. Someone had the smart idea of making sandals, called <u>geta</u>, out of scrap lumber and rope. They are perfect for keeping our feet and hems out of the mud.

P.P.S. You asked about ration books—we don't get those because they cook for us here. But we do get free "coupon books" to be used in our Canteen. Our family gets $5 worth of coupons per month. That wouldn't be so bad if there were better things to buy. How much soap and tooth powder does one family need?

P.P.P.S. Sorry I'm such a grouch. I promise to be more cheerful in my next letter.

GETA

She's hardly a grouch! I would be tons worse. I am going to write to her this minute and tell her so. I'll also tell her she didn't miss much on July 4th. With so many young men enlisting, the parade band sounded pretty pathetic. I sat on the curb where we always sit, in front of Solomon's Deli. A little girl nudged in next to me, in Dottie's usual spot. She had sticky fingers and a piercing scream. Needless to say, I left early.

JULY 8, 1942

Late last night, we heard a crash in our living room. Someone had thrown a rock through our front window, tearing our blackout curtain.

We found this note.

Go back to Germany, Nazi

Just because of our German last name. Mother has to hurry to fix our curtain before tonight so enemy planes won't see our house and bomb us. No one has been bombed here yet, but you never know—and those are government orders. Pop says the Cortinos got a rock through their window because they are Italian. Their note called them Dirty Wops. (The rock thrower is either brave or stupid or both—Mr. Cortino is a policeman!) It made me think: Since America is at war with Germany and Italy, too, how come we aren't locked up in camps like the Japanese?

Look what is happening in Europe.

 **The Seattle B**

Tuesday, July 7, 1942

GERMANY CONQUERS RUSSIAN TOWNS

Adding to holdings in Austria, Czechoslovakia, Poland, Denmark, Norway, Holland, Belgium, France, Yugoslavia and Greece

Pop says Hitler is a madman, trying to take over the world, and there's no way of knowing what terrible things are happening over there.

This came in the mail today from Nick Rossi.

July 6, 1942

Dear Louise,

Thank you for your letter. It really cheered me up! (And smelled good, too.) I made the nurses read it over and over until I had it memorized. I love the socks—all my buddies are jealous. Maybe you can come back and write another letter for me. The nurses here are very busy.

Sincerely,
Seaman Nick Rossi

P.S. My bandages come off in three days. The doctors think with luck, I'll at least be able to see shapes and colors. Cross your fingers.

P.P.S. Don't feel bad about getting sick—it happens to a lot of the new nurses as well. Some of us can't be too swell to look at.

Rats! He heard me! Maybe Pop can save enough gas rations so I can go back and redeem myself. I really want to do my part for the war. Plus, my handwriting is much better than my knitting.

JULY 9, 1942

I found this in our mailbox today.

You are invited to

Nancy Cortino's

14TH BIRTHDAY PARTY,
THURSDAY, AUGUST 6, NOON.

Dear Louise,
   I am sorry for being mean at the movies that time. I hope you will still come to my party.
      Your friend, Nancy Cortino

P.S. Marion is <u>not</u> invited.

Maybe getting a rock through her window has made her a little humbler? Half of me wants to forgive her and go to the party. The other half is still mad. Well, I have a month to decide.

JULY 10, 1942

Guess what? I have joined the Junior Red Cross. We perform lots of important duties for the war effort, like:
* Going house to house collecting cooking grease, aluminum, and tin cans

* Working on a group Victory Garden and helping other people start their own (Ugh, more blisters!)

* Preparing care packages for soldiers

And the main reason I joined:

* First Aid and Disaster Relief training (which I hope will make me braver)

Tomorrow we learn how to make and apply bandages. I wonder how Nick's un-bandaging went. At church I lit one candle for him and one for Dottie's Grumpa. And speaking of Dottie . . .

July 7, 1942

Dear Louise,

Give your mother a tremendous hug from me! People stopped in their tracks to sniff as I walked the sweet-smelling package down to Grumpa. He ate two whole cookies right away. I sat on my hands and tried not to look at the sparkly sugar topping. Your family must have given up a whole year's worth of sugar rations just on that batch.

The cookies gave Grumpa a burst of energy—enough to yell at me about wearing pants. But it's so dirty here, Lou Lou, everyone is wearing them—even some of the prissiest ladies. Robert teases and calls me "Mr. Dottie." I call him "Mr. Invisible."

Mrs. Y decided that I should learn to make tea. It is much more complicated than it sounds. There are about a million different tools and bowls—called dogu—that you have to clean and use in a certain order, in a certain way. (I can't believe Mrs. Y brought them all here—they must have taken up one whole suitcase, and she packed them so carefully that nothing broke!] Before you use each tool or bowl, you must pass it around the table "for your guests to admire." [What guests? The guards?] All this before anyone gets a drop to drink! The whole process takes so long, it's a wonder the entire Japanese population hasn't died off from dehydration. I'm parched just thinking about it.

Yours til the butter flies,
Dottie

P.S. I read that dogs remember people by their smells, so I am sending you my hanky. Please tie it to Roxy's basket. That way, if we ever get out of here, she may still remember me.

"Mr. Invisible"

JULY 11, 1942

Roxy, 5 months old.

I've always read Dottie's letters to her, but now I let her sniff them, too.

Someone smashed the window of Okura's Laundry, even though they sold the store months ago. Werner saw Marion's dad outside the store, laughing. Like father, like daughter.

JULY 15, 1942

Mom says the Hunters (Marion's parents) joined this group. Figures!

JAPANESE

EXCLUSION LEAGUE MEETING

July 17, 8 p.m., Lincoln Square Pavilion

Come voice your opinion

about keeping

America for Americans!

July 13, 1942

Dear Louise,

I'm sorry to hear about the rock through your window. I told my parents about it and Daddy said, "No one is safe from prejudice." Mother just grunted and swept the floor again.

Bad news: Grandfather's flowers died. Mr. Okamoto, the man who runs the Canteen, saw the shriveled plants and laughed. "Don't you know, 'Hana-chan,'" he said, "that nothing but boredom can grow out here?" I wanted to tell him to dry up and blow away. And that MY NAME IS DOTTIE. But my manners won out. Phooey.

I went to visit Grandfather today, and you'll never guess what happened. He was arguing with a nurse, so I stood outside the Infirmary door and waited (okay, I eavesdropped).

"It is all my fault!" he kept yelling. The nurse tried to quiet him, but he just got louder. "For me, an Issei, to be here is okay. I am old and tired. But for Hana-chan, my precious flower, growing up behind barbed wire? No. She is too good for this."

My ears were so full, Lou Lou, I couldn't listen anymore. I ran and hid in the latrine (the one with stalls). It took until dinnertime for my tears to stop flowing. But my heart feels like it will ache forever.

I will never call him Grumpa again.

Yours til the kitchen sinks,
Dottie

P.S. I may have figured out a new plan to help Grandfather. Won't say anything now, as I don't want to jinx it.

P.P.S. An Issei is someone like my grandfather who was born in Japan but came to the US. They can never be US citizens. But Nisei, their children born here, are. My parents are Nisei, and I am third generation, called Sansei. Who knows what my children will be called? Hopefully just "American."

? ? ? ?
?
What could Dottie's plan be?
?
? ? ? ?

My sad
little garden

D.M.

JULY 20, 1942

My knitting has gotten much better. I've made 6 pairs of socks so far and I've even gotten fancy, alternating different colors and stitches. I must send Nick a nicer pair. Maybe something like this. Too bad my artwork hasn't gotten better as well.

It's been two weeks since I wrote to him, asking how his un-bandaging went. Maybe it's bad news and that's why he's not writing back. I prayed for him last night until I fell asleep.

New and Improved socks!

Same size!

Look! No Holes!

No Bumps!

JULY 27, 1942

Terrible news: Werner enlisted in the Navy. That was his secret. Pretty crummy one, in my book. Men between 18 and 65 are required to register for the draft, and those between 18 and 45 are eligible for military service. (Pop is 46—phew!) Couldn't Werner have waited to be called rather than rushing to volunteer? He just turned 18. He leaves for training in about two weeks. Meanwhile, Mother walks around with watery eyes, Pop pats Werner on the back a lot, and I keep having nightmares. In each one, Werner is a patient at the Rehab Hospital. I couldn't even write about it until now. I know I should be proud of him, but it's hard. I'd welcome his teasing all day, every day, if he would just change his mind.

More from Dottie. ⟶

July 25, 1942

Dear Louise,

I'm dashing off this note to you while I wait in line at the Mess Hall. Grandfather has lost 2 more pounds, so I'm spending every spare second working on my special plan for him. I can't believe your brother joined the Navy! Your mother must be terribly sad. There are rumors scooting around camp that soon the government will allow our boys to enlist, too. Cousin Albert and his buddies are over the moon—it's all they talk about. Uncle Taro is back to foaming at the mouth, and Aunt Etsu is so upset she's sewn more curtains than she knows what to do with. For once, I agree with the adults—it doesn't seem fair that our boys should fight for America but can't live as free Americans.

Last night, there was a dance at the Mess Hall. No musicians but several radios, all tuned to the same big band station. Near the end, when "Stardust" came on and all the couples began slow dancing, Mrs. Y inched her way out to the middle and began a traditional Japanese dance! One by one, people backed up to watch. At first, I was embarrassed for her. But oh, Lou Lou! When Louie Armstrong sang about each kiss being an inspiration, Mrs. Y hid behind her fan, looking 20 years old. Watching her dance, I could see the bright stars Mr. Armstrong sang of and even hear the nightingale telling his fairy tale.

By the time the song ended and she'd bowed her head, my skin was covered in goose bumps. The radios blared out a new song, but nobody moved. Finally, Robert Fujiu started clapping, and then everyone was clapping and smiling big smiles. Someone yelled, "Curfew!" and we all ran home. But even lying on my cot in all that inky blackness, I could still see Mrs. Yatsushiro dancing and dancing.

Now I'm at the front of the chow line, so I'd better go.

Grr, gurgle, growl, grumble (hungry stomach language for <u>See you later, alligator</u>).

Dottie

See Ya Later!

I sure wish I could've seen Mrs. Y dance. It sounds beautiful.

AUGUST 5, 1942

Empty toothpaste tubes have to be saved and returned in order to purchase "refills." So Mother now buys the powdered kind. It's like brushing your teeth with sand—yuck! It's strange all these everyday things you never think about until they're gone. I learned in Junior Red Cross that the tin cans we collect are used to make tiny tubes with needles on the ends, called "syrettes." They're filled with medicine and used on the battlefield to prevent shock in wounded soldiers. Nick probably knows all about those. Hopefully Werner won't.

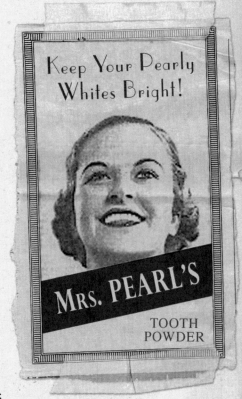

Keep Your Pearly Whites Bright!

MRS. PEARL'S

TOOTH POWDER

AUGUST 6, 1942

As you can see, I did end up going to Nancy's party. I wasn't planning on it and then wouldn't you know, Pastor Mael's sermon this week was on forgiveness, and I swear he kept glancing in my direction. I gave Nancy hankies with

Party Streamer:

N embroidered (by me) in the corners. She said she was sorry again, and I said I forgave her. But I think it will take a long time before my heart feels the words my mouth said.

I brought home a slice of cake for Werner, as he is leaving tomorrow.

August 2, 1942

Dear Louise,

You asked for a hint about my secret project, so I'll give you two:

1) Mrs. Y is teaching me . . .

2) It's giving me lots of paper cuts.

Fortunately, our work leaves no time for wiping out tea bowls or admiring tea scoops. Unfortunately, we still have to sit seiza, but I don't mind so much anymore. I've even found myself sitting that way without realizing it!

Robert Fujiu said something strange the other day. We'd been talking about The Little Princess, with Shirley Temple (or rather, Robert had been talking about it, and it was putting me in a bad mood). Finally, he said, "What's wrong with you?" I told him, "Nothing," but Robert can badger you until you're ready to die. "Fine!" I yelled. "I'll never look like Shirley Temple, okay?!" I don't know which one of us was more surprised.

Before the war, Lou Lou, I never thought about my looks. I mean, I knew I had black hair and almond eyes, but I felt I looked like everyone else. Now I see my face in all the political cartoons and war posters—Uncle Sam pointing his finger at me, saying, "Jap, you're next!" Every time I look in the mirror, I feel ashamed.

But Robert must see things differently. Because after I came out with that Shirley Temple remark, he said, "Too bad for her. <u>She'll</u> never look like <u>you</u>!" Then he shoved his best baseball card—a 1942 Ted Williams—into my hand and ran off. The card was still warm. I didn't add it to my stack, though. I put it up next to my picture of you and Roxy. Seeing it there makes me feel good, and I'm not even much of a baseball fan.

Stay tuned to your mailbox for the further adventures of . . . "Dottie Goes to Puyallup."

XOXOXO,
D

P.S. I am thinking about Werner and praying for his safety.

Mrs. Y + paper cuts = ?

Is this what "real Americans" look like?

"We'll have lots to eat this winter, won't we Mother?"

**Grow your own
Can your own**

AUGUST 7, 1942

Speaking of Shirley Temple, Nancy invited me to see <u>Miss</u>
<u>Annie Rooney</u>, but I didn't feel like going. Nancy talked the manager
into giving her this lobby card since it was frayed, and then she
gave it to me! (I think she's still trying to make up for being
mean about Dottie.)

Anyway, Nancy said Shirley jitterbugged and had her first
on-screen kiss by Dickie Moore. I tried to act enthusiastic for
Nancy's sake, but my heart wasn't in it. I miss Werner already
and he only left this morning. Mother is still crying. What if

something happens to him? I am now praying without ceasing. I guess it is possible, after all.

Pop's going back to Sasser Facial Rehab soon for a follow-up story and asked if I wanted to go. I do, and I don't. What if I embarrass myself again? Will Nick still be there? What if he's not? He STILL hasn't written me back! I feel like my whole summer has been spent waiting by the mailbox.

AUGUST 16, 1942

We got our first letter from Werner! He is well, has already made a best friend by the name of George, and says he misses us all. "Especially you, squirt," he wrote, meaning me. But my bad dreams continue. Last night I dreamt his face was covered in blood and he was yelling, "You're next, Jap!" at Dottie's cousin Albert. It took me a long time to get back to sleep.

This morning I started on a pair of socks for Werner, using Mother's best yarn. Being productive is making me feel a little better—I'm busy counting stitches instead of minutes. Still, I wish I could make Werner something that would keep him safe instead of just warm.

Piece of Pop's shoe, courtesy of Roxy. $\longrightarrow$

Mother is furious. Leather shoes are so hard to come by, with all the boots that have to be made for the soldiers.

But I can't bring myself to scold Roxy—she's probably missing Dottie as much as I am. Look how big she is now!

AUGUST 20, 1942

I did it—I went back to Sasser! And those nightmares I've been having about Werner actually <u>helped.</u> Walking in, I realized every soldier there was <u>somebody</u>'s brother. And then I wanted to help them all. I wrote letters for five soldiers before I worked up the courage to visit Nick. He grinned when he heard my voice (he remembered it!) but then immediately covered his eyes, one of which was purple and swollen and criss-crossed with stitches. Do you know what? It didn't bother me one whit! And guess what he told me? "You're a sight for sore eyes." We had a good laugh over that one. He can see shapes, light, and even some colors. He says the doctors are hopeful for continued healing.

After I wrote his letter, we sat and talked. Nick told me he is 17, only 3 years older than me! He lied about his age to enlist. I'm a bit embarrassed about how much I told him—about Pop's article on Sasser, Werner enlisting, Roxy's latest exploits, and even news from Dottie. When I mentioned she was in an internment camp, his smile faded. "She's Japanese, then," he said.

And before I even realized it, Dottie's words flew out of my mouth: "No, she's <u>American</u>!" Suddenly, I felt very hot. "American, with . . . Japanese roots," I mumbled.

Nick turned his head away and said, "My ship, the <u>Lexington</u>, was attacked by Japanese torpedoes. And dive-bombers. That's how I ended up . . . like this."

I flipped the pen I was holding over and over in my hands. Finally, I said, "Nick, isn't your last name Italian?" He didn't answer. Then I said, "And my last name, <u>Krueger</u>, well, you can't get more German than that." I wasn't sure what to say next. But then Pop was there, telling me it was time to go. When I stood up, Nick put out his hand and we shook. I couldn't tell if it was a "see you next time" shake or a "good-bye forever" one. There was so much I wanted to tell him, to explain. But all I could come up with was, "You'd like Dottie. I know it."

He hates me? He hates me not?

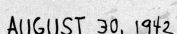

AUGUST 30, 1942

Roxy, lucky to be almost 7 months old.

When it rains, Dad comes home with one wet foot, thanks to the holes in his shoe.

Dottie's been gone over four months now. Next week I start at Jefferson High. Dottie and I should be going there _together_! Every year, on the first day of school, we wear at least one thing that matches. One time our mothers let us buy the same cardigan sweater—other years, it was just a bracelet or lacy socks. This year, since money's tight, I bought us both plaid hair ribbons. I sent Dottie hers last week, with instructions to wear it next Tuesday. She'd better! Nancy and most of my old classmates from Washington will be going to Jefferson, but it won't be the same without Dottie. (Oh and get this—Marion is going to a _private school_ called Fillmore Academy. Figures. As Mother says, good riddance to bad rubbish!)

SEPTEMBER 10, 1942

Well, what do you know? I passed my Junior Red Cross class. I got the highest score! ☆

Nurse Meyer, my instructor, said I should think about becoming a nurse, too—me, Little Miss Scaredy Pants. Could I ever be

THE AMERICAN NATIONAL RED CROSS

THIS IS TO CERTIFY THAT _Louise Krueger_

HAS SUCCESSFULLY PASSED THE _First Aid Training_ COURSE

OF THE JUNIOR RED CROSS _Bainbridge Island Chapter_

September 5, 1942

Angela Meyer, R.N.

brave enough? Or smart enough? Or keep my mouth shut long

enough, so as not to upset the patients?

No word from Nick. He's probably dropped me like a hot potato.

September 7, 1942

Dear Louise,

Terrible news and wonderful news. We're getting out of here. But before you start thinking that's the wonderful news, read on: We are going to another camp, farther away, but they haven't told us where yet. I'll write you as soon as I know. Oh Lou Lou, will I ever get home?

And now for the wonderful part—last night, Mrs. Y and I finished my secret project. So today, right after school, I walked into the Infirmary, hiding it behind my back. Grandfather barely noticed me. Then, with my heart galloping like a hundred wild horses, I placed my project onto his bed. Ta-da! It's a window box overflowing with flowers—red roses, white lilies, yellow tulips, and one cherry blossom branch.

"They're origami," I said, in case it wasn't clear. Grandfather slowly nodded. "Daddy made the window box, and Mrs. Y taught me how to make the different flowers."

(Origami is an art where you make things out of paper—you have to fold a single sheet, without cutting or gluing or taping. I think Miss Murret would like it! I drew a picture, so you can see.)

After what seemed like an awfully long time, Grandfather whispered, "Did my American granddaughter make these?"

I bowed and answered, "No, your Japanese American granddaughter did."

Then, without taking his eyes off the flowers, he reached over. "Thank you . . . Dottie," he said, giving my hand a squeeze.

"Do itashimashite," I answered, which means "Don't mention it."
Only I don't think I said it right because Grandfather
laughed until little tears dripped out of the corners of his
wrinkled eyes.

I saved my favorite flower for you, Lou Lou, so you won't
forget me. (You haven't, have you? I thought maybe after
that first visit, your family would come again. Maybe when
we get to our new camp?) The little red tulip is for Roxy—
could you put it on her collar? Having her with you, it's
almost like a little part of me is with you, too.

Friends 4-ever?

Dorothy Hana-chan Masuoka

(Hana means flower. Mrs. Y told me that!)

P.S. I hear you are good friends with Nancy Cortino now?
P.P.S. Remember Grant,
Remember Lee,
The heck with them,
Remember me!

Nancy and I are friendly but not "good" friends. I wonder who she heard that from. I'd never drop Dottie for Nancy. Best friends never forget! I'm writing to tell her so. Hopefully my letter will make it there before she leaves. Where is she going next? What if it's too far to visit? She's right. I should have tried to visit again at Puyallup. It's just . . . hard to see her there.

SEPTEMBER 20, 1942

Here is my new school schedule:

1. American History
2. Algebra
3. Literature Through the Ages
4. Lunch/Study
5. Typing
6. Physical Science
7. Gym
8. Music and the Arts

Literature is my favorite subject—however, Mrs. Singleton "tsk-tsked" when she saw my copy of The Haunted Bridge, sitting on top of Romeo and Juliet. "Miss Krueger," she said, sniffing, "I hardly think Nancy Drew Mysteries are worthy of your attention." (It's amazing how any words get out through that pursed mouth of hers.) I don't care. Dottie and I will still be reading Nancy Drew books when we're 80!

High school is the bee's knees. The teachers treat you more like adults. But the work is <u>hard</u>! I wonder if Dottie has a separate high school in her new camp or if they're all just squished together like before. I haven't heard back from her. Did they move yet? I wonder if she got my last letter.

SEPTEMBER 21, 1942

Look what arrived today.

September 17, 1942

Dear Louise,

Thank you for your visit and for writing letters to all our parents. They really worry about us, and the letters ease their minds.

I'm afraid I have to apologize for two things—first, for not writing you back sooner. I wanted to wait until I healed more and didn't look so much like Frankenstein's monster. When you came in, I was pretty embarrassed. But then we got to having such a nice time, I completely forgot about how I looked.

The second apology is more complicated. You must think I hate all Japanese. But I don't. Well, I don't anymore. You see, after our ship was bombed, I woke up in the water—blind, bleeding, and drowning. Luckily, two of my buddies pulled me onto some floating wreckage and after many hours, we were picked up by one of our destroyers. Lying on the deck of that ship, I realized I was actually going to live. Then the destroyer spotted a downed Japanese airman clinging to a piece of tail section. I could hear the soldiers on board yelling to him and thought for sure we'd pick him up.

But we <u>didn't</u>. A few minutes later, we heard a big boom, and the airman's wreckage was in flames. Some guys said it was a fuel leak. Others said the airman was booby-trapped and would have blown us up if we'd rescued him. I guess we'll never know. But out of all the horrible things I experienced during my short tour, the thought of that airman bobbing around in the vast ocean, injured and alone, is what haunts me most. When I heard your best friend was Japanese, all I could think of was him.

Sorry for getting so dark (my third apology). I do hope you can come back soon. With a bit of luck, I will look a heck of a lot better by then. And speaking of looks, a few of the guys here say you are much too pretty for the likes of me. I believe it!

Very Sincerely Yours,
Seaman Nick Rossi

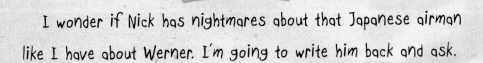

I wonder if Nick has nightmares about that Japanese airman like I have about Werner. I'm going to write him back and ask.

SEPTEMBER 25, 1942

Another letter from Werner! He says he expects to be shipped out very soon but can't say much more. "Loose Lips Sink Ships" is the motto. Pop convinced Mother to let me put this in my scrapbook.

All soldiers wear "dog tags" with their important information on them. Here's a rubbing of mine. My "service number" is the long one. Then comes next of kin, address, and religion. We're told never to take them off.

```
KRUEGER, WERNER M.
13496623 T42 42 A
GEORGE KRUEGER
505 CRESCENT ST
BAINBRIDGE ISLAND WA P
```

I'm going to save my pennies for a chocolate bar to send. They say soldiers appreciate cigarettes and sweets the most. (Werner doesn't smoke!) To keep from worrying, I'm busying myself with Junior Red Cross projects and activities at Jefferson High—I've joined the school newspaper. Like father, like daughter, I suppose.

OCTOBER 5, 1942

The St. Louis Cardinals beat the New York Yankees in the World Series. I wish I could get Dottie an Enos Slaughter card. Pop says he's the best player on the Cardinals, "with a batting average of .318." Whatever that means.

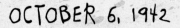

OCTOBER 6, 1942

Roxy, 8 months.

How big is this dog going to get? Dottie won't even recognize her when she gets back. <u>If</u> she gets back. Still no word about her move, and it's been almost one whole month since her last letter!

OCTOBER 29, 1942

Haven't written much this month—guess I kind of lost steam when Dottie stopped writing. I check the mailbox every day but haven't heard a word from her. I've also been busy with school and the Junior Red Cross. Here's something—our group's Victory Garden was a big success. The total harvest (in number of bushel baskets) was: 15 zucchinis, 13 tomatoes, 12 lettuces, 12 potatoes, 9 spinach, 8 1/2 green beans, 6 carrots, and 5 onions. We brought our fresh vegetables by wagon to a different church every week, where they were distributed to needy families in the area.

Here is my badge of honor.

I call it the Green Thumb Award. The last thing to be harvested were pumpkins—filling 7 wagons! We are bringing them to St. Norbert's Orphanage tomorrow.

NOVEMBER 1, 1942

Because of the war, Halloween "tricks" and "treats" were scarce this year. No potatoes in exhaust pipes, no soap on windows, no Vaseline on door handles. I guess even tricksters would rather eat the potato than listen for the "bang" when their unsuspecting neighbor starts up his car. (And cars are used so much less— they may have had a long wait!) While there were few sweets, carving pumpkins for the orphans was all the treat I needed. 6-year-old Martha insisted her pumpkin have sharp teeth, frowning eyebrows, and . . . roller skates? It was hard not to laugh. And even harder to leave.

I wonder what Dottie did for Halloween? It's been nearly two months since I've heard from her! She can't still be mad because I'm friendly with Nancy Cortino? So what could have happened? I've written three letters to Dottie's old address at Camp Harmony with the words "PLEASE FORWARD" in big capital letters and still nothing.

Pop always says, "If you want to get things done, go to the top." So I also wrote to Milton Eisenhower, Director of the War Relocation Authority, and asked him where the Masuokas were transferred. I mentioned he might want to work on improving their mail delivery system. I've vowed to write to him twice a week until I hear something. Meanwhile, Pop is using all his contacts, and Mother is asking everyone we know.

NOVEMBER 16, 1942

Five letters to Milton Eisenhower and no word from him or Dottie. **WHERE IS SHE???**

She'd better write back soon, as I am running out of pages. If I'd known Dottie was going to be gone this long, I would've bought a larger book.

NOVEMBER 30, 1942

I've now sent Mr. Eisenhower ten letters and have heard nothing. Mother is furious about how many stamps I've used. I don't care. Dottie is worth every penny.

No word from Werner or Nick, either. Maybe the entire US Postal System has gone kerflooey.

Last week was Thanksgiving. Mother tried to make it nice, but none of us were in a celebrating mood. I couldn't even look at the pumpkin pie, remembering how Werner and I always fight over the first piece. Pop ended up bringing it to the orphanage, where it was gobbled up in no time. For that, I was thankful.

DECEMBER 9, 1942

Finally! A response from the War Relocation Authority! Although it's not much. Dottie will be 30 by the time they find her!

December 5, 1942

Dear Miss Krueger,

We have received all of your letters. Rest assured we are

looking into the situation. However, this is a lengthy process

as we have over 100,000 people of Japanese descent in our

camps. We request your patience during this time of war.

Thank you.

OFFICE OF THE WAR RELOCATION AUTHORITY Washington, DC

DECEMBER 17, 1942

One piece of good news: Nick was released from Sasser!

December 12, 1942

Dear Louise,

Returning home to Wyoming was swell—it's been great to
see family and friends. I'm going a bit stir-crazy now, with my
mother fussing over me. She follows me around the house,
pulling shades, dimming lights, thinking anything and everything I
do will make my sight worse. I don't have the strength to
make it through a full day of school yet, so my principal
arranged to have me tutored to finish my senior year. I was
never much of a student, Louise, but I must say, those
sessions are now the highlight of my day!

I go through low times, too, mostly when I think of my
buddies who died, as well as the ones that are still out there
fighting. I wish I could go back and join them but because of
my eyes, I can't. I received an Honorable Discharge as well as
a Purple Heart, though I really don't feel like I deserved it. In
case you've never seen one, I did a rubbing for you.

I still think of that Japanese airman every day. I really don't know how I'll ever get that memory out of my mind. My whole family knows about him because I wake up screaming some nights. In my dreams, I'm always in a boat and hear a scratching noise down below. I know it's him, trapped underneath. I think my screams scare my kid sister more than my face does. And that's pretty scary! Ha, ha.

Anyway, from now on, you can write to me at the address on the back of this envelope. Maybe you could include your phone number in your next letter—it would be nice to hear your voice again. Have you any word from your brother? Where is he stationed? And how about your friend Dottie? How is she faring?

I hope to hear from you soon.

Yours truly,

Nick

P.S. My one eye has improved so much, I'm now able to read your letters by myself.

So he's having nightmares, too. But he's with his family now. They must be so relieved to have him home. I know I'd be over the moon if Werner came back, even injured, because at least he'd be alive. I do wish Nick lived close by, though. Wyoming is forever away. I wonder if I'll ever see him again?

DECEMBER 18, 1942

<u>Still</u> no word from Dottie. (I wrote a follow-up letter to my pal Mr. Eisenhower so he knows he can't forget me. I'm going to badger him more than Robert badgers Dottie.) And no word from Werner. Pop says, "No news is good news." But when I see Pop staring out our front window, I know he's worried, too.

DECEMBER 21, 1942

HUGE news! And Pop heard through his sources that <u>my letters</u> initiated this investigation!

POST OFFICE WORKER ACCUSED OF MAIL TAMPERING

POST OFFICE EMPLOYEE Victor Hunter was accused by an unnamed coworker of stealing and destroying mail. The informant alleges that Mr. Hunter bragged about confiscating and burning mail arriving from and going out to various Japanese internment camps across the West. "I know who the Jap-lovers are," Mr. Hunter told the coworker, "and I refuse to let them endanger my country." Mr. Hunter is currently being held for questioning.

This must be why I haven't heard from Dottie! And Dottie probably hasn't gotten my letters, either. Maybe she's written me scads of times and wondered why I never wrote back. Oh, I hope, hope, _hope_ she tries to write me again!

Imagine, Mr. Hunter, Marion's father! The whole neighborhood is talking about it. But something strange has happened: There's a little part of me feeling sorry for Marion. I mean, you can't help who your parents are, can you?

DECEMBER 24, 1942

And now for two of the best Christmas presents ever. . . . First, a telegram from Werner.

THE COMPANY WILL APPRECIATE SUGGESTIONS FROM ITS PATRONS CONCERNING ITS SERVICE   1204

WESTERN UNION

CLASS OF SERVICE	SIGNS
This is a full-rate Telegram or Cablegram unless its deferred character is indicated by a suitable sign above or preceding the address.	DL = Day Letter
	NM = Night Message
	NL = Night Letter
	LC = Deferred Cable
	NLT = Cable Night Letter
	Ship Radiogram

R. B. WHITE
PRESIDENT

NEWCOMB CARLTON
CHAIRMAN OF THE BOARD

J. C. WILLEVER
FIRST VICE-PRESIDENT

The filing time as shown in the date line on full-rate telegrams and day letters, and the time of receipt at destination as shown on all messages, is STANDARD TIME.

Received at December 24, 1942   3 32 PM

MERRY CHRISTMAS. GOT PROMOTED TO AERM. AM WELL AND HAVING TURKEY DINNER. MISS YOU TONS. LOVE WERNER

After all this time, wouldn't you think he could write more than 17 words? Oh, but they are the most beautiful 17 words in the world! (Pop says AERM stands for Aerographer's Mate, which means Werner watches and records the weather using various instruments. In my next letter, I'm going to tell him to get his head out of the clouds! Ha, ha.)

And then this.

December 22, 1942

Dear Louise,

Merry Christmas to you and your family. I hope you've heard from Werner by now and that he's safe and well. I told you a little about my kid sister and how worried she was about me, right? Well, over toast this morning, she said, "You can't really forget a memory, Nick. But you _can_ replace it with a nicer one."

So, do you know what she did? Volunteered me to accompany Mom's church ladies on their annual Christmas Gift Drop. Guess where? Heart Mountain Relocation Center, about 30 miles from our home (I didn't even know it was there). Louise, I'm not sure who was more nervous and grateful—the old, sick Japanese man I gave the gift basket to, or me.

Your friend,
Nick

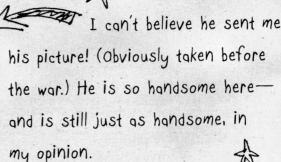

I can't believe he sent me his picture! (Obviously taken before the war.) He is so handsome here—and is still just as handsome, in my opinion.

JANUARY 3, 1943

What a way to start the New Year! (And with just a few pages left in my book!)

December 27, 1942

Dear Louise,

After you stopped answering my letters, I was afraid our friendship was over. And then we found out about Mr. Hunter and what he did. Have you been writing all along? Did you even know where to send your letters?

These last few months have been the hardest. Cousin Albert enlisted, my grandfather got pneumonia, and on top of all that, I thought you had given me up as a friend. I was so happy to hear about Mr. Hunter burning our mail! I got some strange looks, Lou Lou, when people saw me jumping up and down at the news!

You'll never guess who's been the biggest help to me through these tough times—Robert. He's grown up a lot being in here. And in more ways than one. He's gotten so tall, he practically towers over me now. Not so invisible anymore!

Please write as soon as you get this. We are at Heart Mountain Relocation Center in Wyoming. We don't know how long we will be here, but I think it will be quite a while.

Yours til the horse flies,
    the board walks,
        and the sun sets,

            Dottie

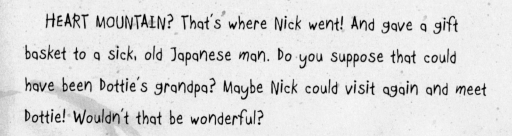

HEART MOUNTAIN? That's where Nick went! And gave a gift basket to a sick, old Japanese man. Do you suppose that could have been Dottie's grandpa? Maybe Nick could visit again and meet Dottie! Wouldn't that be wonderful?

JANUARY 5, 1943

My legs could not carry me fast enough to the Post Office—even in the pouring rain—to mail my next letter to Dottie. Neither snow nor rain nor heat nor gloom of night could stop this best friend!

I included a friendship pledge to sign and return.

I can barely stand the wait.

JANUARY 10, 1943

Here it is! Signed in ink, even by Roxy. ♡

We, the undersigned, renew our pledge to be

Best Friends FOREVER!

<u>Louise Krueger</u>   <u>Dottie Masuoka</u>

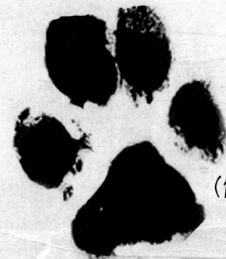

(Roxy Masuoka)

Though there are still so many things I don't know: Will Werner return safely? Will I ever see Nick again? When will this horrible war end? When will Dottie come home? There is one thing I do know for certain: Whether we're around the corner or around the world, Dottie and I will be friends <u>forever</u>.

AUTHOR'S NOTE

In her scrapbook, Louise says it all began with Japan bombing Pearl Harbor. But it didn't just happen out of the blue. With few natural resources of its own, Japan had been invading China and Korea for years and had plans to expand its empire throughout the East Indies and Southeast Asia. The US, with its huge fleet of ships in Pearl Harbor and naval bases on Guam and Wake islands, was the only country capable of stopping these plans. In an effort to disable the American navy, Japan took the offensive, starting with the bombing at Pearl Harbor on December 7, 1941. Over 2,400 American military personnel and civilians were killed and approximately 1,280 were wounded.

Japan's plan of immobilizing the US Navy did not work as well as they'd hoped. In fact, Japanese Imperial Admiral Yamamoto is rumored to have said, "I fear we have awakened a sleeping giant and filled him with a terrible resolve." The day following the attack on Pearl Harbor, the US declared war on Japan.

Suddenly, Americans living on the West Coast felt vulnerable and afraid. If Japan attacked Hawaii, they thought, surely

California, Oregon, and Washington would be next. It occurred to many that the large Japanese American population living in those states might feel a loyalty to their homeland and become spies or saboteurs for Japan. Fueled by this fear, various solutions were explored until one stuck—placing people of Japanese heritage behind barbed wire. On February 19, 1942, President Roosevelt signed Executive Order 9066, which set the stage for the forced removal and incarceration of anyone General De Witt, of the Western Defense Command, thought a menace to the West Coast, which ended up including Americans of Japanese, German, and Italian descent. Those of Japanese heritage were by far the most widely affected.

Three days after Pearl Harbor, Germany and Italy declared war on the US as well. World War II had begun. The fighting went on for over three years when, on May 7, 1945, Germany formally surrendered to the Allies (the British Empire, USSR, and the US), ending the war in Europe. Japan signed their surrender agreement on September 2, 1945, after suffering two devastating atomic bombings by the US in Hiroshima and Nagasaki. It is estimated that over 220,000 Japanese people died as a result of those bombings, and the long-term radiation effects are still being studied. This is the only use of atomic weapons in warfare to date. By the time World War II was over, somewhere between forty and sixty million people, from fifty-eight different countries, had lost their lives. Of those deaths, close to two-thirds were civilians.

Beginning in 1943, some Japanese American internees were allowed to leave the camps to attend college or work. Others didn't leave until the bans against resettlement of the West Coast were removed in 1945. Tule Lake was the last internment camp to close, on March 20, 1946. Although many former internees reported a satisfactory resettlement, others had just the opposite experience, with their homes, farms, and businesses gone or people speaking out against their return.

For these reasons, internees were encouraged to restart their lives "inland," in cities such as Chicago or Denver where prejudice was not as high. Some educated and formerly respected Japanese American professionals were forced to take low-paying jobs as babysitters or store clerks to begin their new lives. It must have seemed to these individuals that their humiliation would never end. Though not physically mistreated, the American Japanese had been stripped of their rights, their freedom, their property, and maybe most importantly, their dignity.

The first step toward conquering anti-Japanese prejudice occurred one year after the war ended. In 1946, President Harry S. Truman honored the most decorated American regiment from WWII—the all-Japanese American 442nd Regimental Combat Team. In a White House lawn ceremony, the president told the surviving soldiers, "You fought not only the enemy but you fought prejudice—and you have won."

After many years of discussion, President Ronald Reagan signed a law in 1988 providing $20,000 to each surviving internee and $1.25 billion toward an education fund. On October 9, 1990, Reverend Momoru Etu, 107 years old, received the first check.

Although Dottie and Louise and their families are fictional characters, others, such as Eddie Sato and Milton Eisenhower, were real people. Many elements in this story were factual or based on fact (such as the trays of fake eyeballs, the Camp Harmony News-Letter, Victory Gardens, the Exclusion League and exclusion orders, etc). Other elements, such as Victor Hunter's mail tampering and the downed Japanese airman story, were products of my imagination. The artwork was created as accurately as research allowed, though modifications were made to avoid trademark infringements or for editorial or design needs. For example, The Seattle Beacon, the Junior Red Cross certificate, Spring's Best oleo, and Mrs. Pearls Tooth Powder were my own inventions. Some items were altered for layout purposes. It's also important to note that Bainbridge Island residents were actually ordered to be evacuated on or around March 23, 1942, and sent to Manzanar, not Camp Harmony. I changed this for the purposes of the story.

Beverly Patt

THANKS . . .

* First and foremost to Dave and Margaret Masuoka, who shared, through countless e-mails, letters, and phone calls, what life in the camps was really like. And thanks to Brett and Lynn Masuoka for introducing us!

* To Roger W. Lotchin, Professor of History, Department of History, University of North Carolina-Chapel Hill, for his expert review of the text and artwork.

* To those who allowed us to use their photos (in order of appearance): my mom, Joan Lyle (Louise); Margaret Masuoka (Dottie); my uncle Jim (Werner); Anne McElfresh (Marion); and my father, Gale Lyle (Nick Rossi). Special thanks to Anne, who, I'm told, is as kind as Marion was mean.

* To fellow writers, Mary Ann Bumbera, Marlene Donnelly, Esther Hershenhorn, Cynthea Liu, Jude Mandell, Sarah Roggio, Tammi Sauer, Sara Shacter, Ruth Spiro, Bev Spooner, and Kim Winters, many of whom have helped this manuscript go from a small collection of cryptic letters to its final form.

* To Tanya Dean, whose invaluable input and enthusiasm helped me bring this manuscript to a new level.

* To Alyssa Eisner Henkin, for negotiating the contract.

* To my editor, Robin Benjamin, for her wise and patient guidance.

* To illustrator (and new friend) Shula Klinger, for her beautiful sketches and paintings, to designer Kristen Branch, for the incredible feat of making this book look even better than it did in my imagination, and to everyone at Marshall Cavendish, for making this dream of mine such a beautiful reality.

* To the Japanese American Museum and their extensive collection documenting the Japanese American experience.

* To the University of Washington Library, with their incredible online Camp Harmony exhibit.

* To Vaux Toneff, for sharing her experiences at a California facial rehab hospital and for finding a willing "Marion."

* To my in-laws, Ken and Jeanne Patt, for scouring their memory banks when I'd phone at odd hours, asking about the price of butter in 1942 or how a sailor might get hit with shrapnel but not die.

* To Keely, Owen, Shayna, and Mason, for putting up with empty sock drawers and overcooked dinners.

* And to my loving and supportive husband, Jerry, who has believed in me all along.

BIBLIOGRAPHY

"Bainbridge Island." *Washington State Library*. 20 August 2000.
   http://www.lib.washington.edu/exhibits/harmony/Exhibit/bainbridge.html.

"Building a Community Under Crisis." *Colorado State Library*. 12
   November 2003. http://www.colostate.edu/Orgs/TuleLake/Crisis.html.

"Camp Harmony News-Letter," Vol. 1, No. 6. Puyallup, WA, June 12,
   1942. *Washington State Library*. 20 August 2000.
   http://www.lib.washington.edu/exhibits/harmony/Newsletter/1-6.html.

"Civil Liberties." *Washington State Library*. 20 August 2000.
   http://www.lib.washington.edu/exhibits/harmony/Exhibit/civil.html.

"Housing." *Washington State Library*. 20 August 2000.
   http://www.lib/washington.edu/exhibits/harmony/Exhibit/housing.html.

Houston, Jeanne Wakatsuki and James D. Houston. *Farewell to
   Manzanar*. New York: Bantam Books, 1973.

Iki, Darcie C. "Disrupted Lives, Fragmented History." *Japanese
   American National Museum Magazine*. Spring 2000: 9-12.

Jackson, Paul. *The Complete Origami Course*. New York: Smith
   Publishing, 1989.

Japanese American Internment: A Historical Reader. Evanston, IL:
   McDougal Littell, 2000.

Kneibler, Irmgard. *Creative Origami*. Germany: Ottenheimer, 1991.

Masuoka, Dave and Margaret. Telephone, E-mail, and Letter
   Interviews, April 2000—Sept 2003.

"Miss Evanson's Class." *Washington State Library*. 20 August 2000.
   http://www.lib.washington.edu/exhibits/harmony/Exhibit/children.html.

Niiya, Brian. *Japanese American History: An A-to-Z Reference from
   1868 to the Present*. Los Angeles, CA: Japanese American National
   Museum, 1997.

"Pearl Harbor." *Encarta Online Encyclopedia, 2003*. 12 October 2003.

  http://encarta.msn.com/encnet/refpages/RefArticle.aspx?refid+761569623.

"Physical Layout." *Washington State Library*. 20 August 2000.

  http://www.lib.washington.edu/exhibits/harmony/Exhibit/layout.html.

Simon, Richard. "Internment Sites Preservation." *Owens Valley

  History*. 8 August 2007.

  http://www.owensvalleyhistory.com/manzanar3/page13.html.

Stanley, Jerry. *I Am an American*. New York: Crown Publishers, 1994.

"The Japanese Tea Ceremony (Chaji)." *Holy Mountain*. 19 December

  2006. http://www.holymtn.com/tea/Japanesetea.htm.

Yancey, Diane. *Life in a Japanese Internment Camp*. San Diego, CA:

  Lucent Books, 1998.

"1942 in History." *Brainy History*. 25 February 2008.

  http://www.brainyhistory.com/years/1942/html.